DAYDREAMERS

DAYDREAMERS

Tom Feelings Eloise Greenfield

Dial Books for Young Readers
 New York

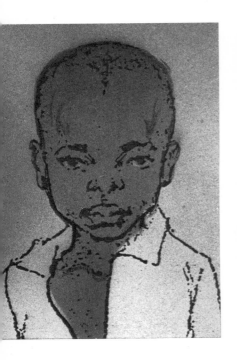

Dial Books for Young Readers
2 Park Avenue
New York, New York 10016

Library of Congress Catalog Card Number: 80-27262
First Pied Piper Printing 1985
Printed in Hong Kong by South China Printing Co.
COBE
4 6 8 10 9 7 5 3
A Pied Piper Book is a registered trademark of
Dial Books for Young Readers,
a division of NAL Penguin Inc.,
® TM 1,163,686 and ® TM 1,054,312.

DAYDREAMERS
is published in a hardcover edition by
Dial Books for Young Readers.
ISBN 0-8037-0167-5

For my sister Flo, who used to carry
this daydreamer on her back.

T.F.

For Stephanie Blocker

E.G.

Daydreamers . . .

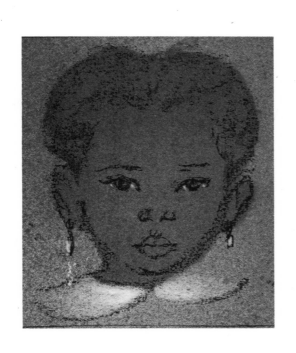

holding their bodies still
for a time
letting the world turn around them

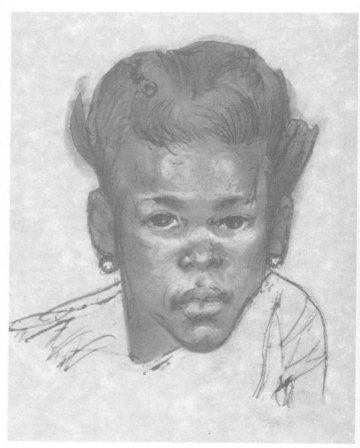

while their dreams hopscotch,
doubledutch, dance,

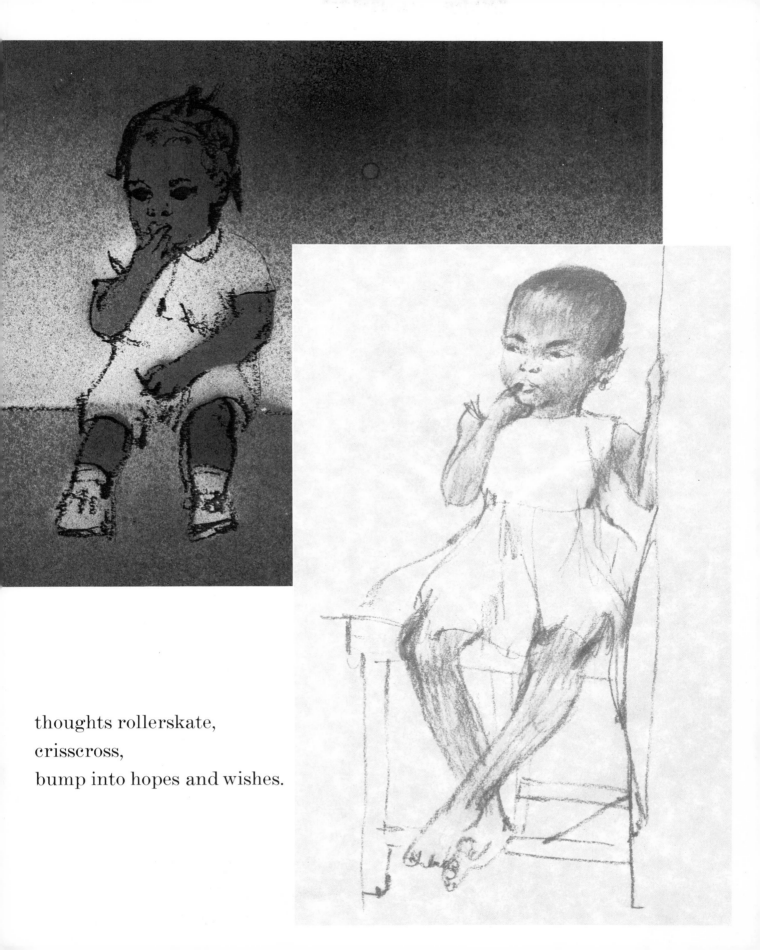

thoughts rollerskate,
crisscross,
bump into hopes and wishes.

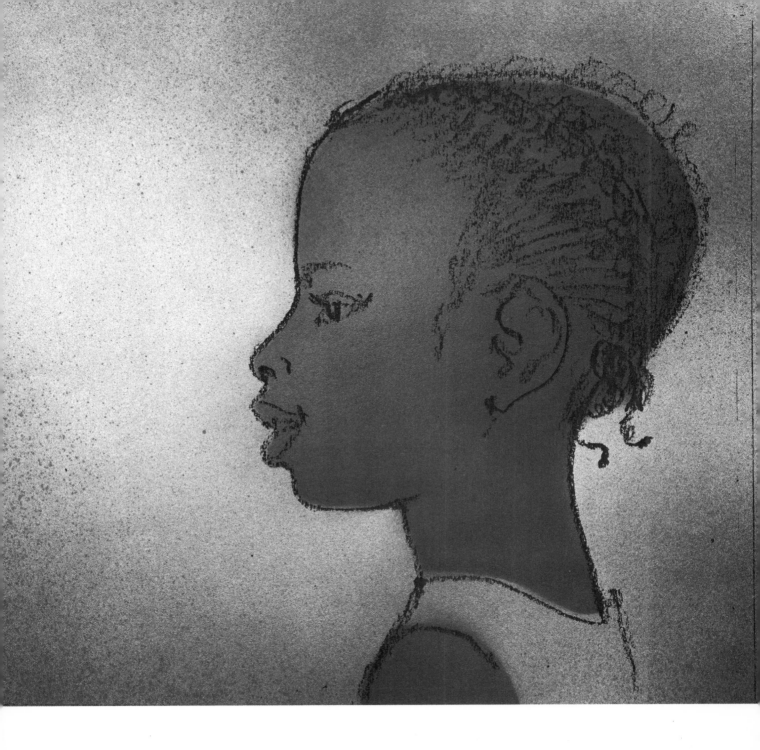

Dreamers
thinking up new ways,
looking toward new days,

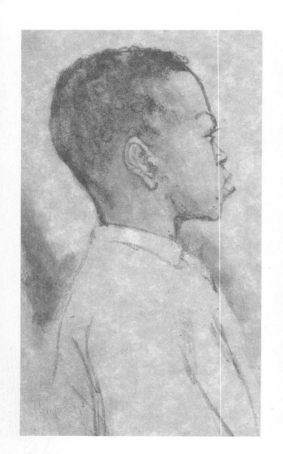

planning new tries,
asking new whys.
Before long,
hands will start to move again,

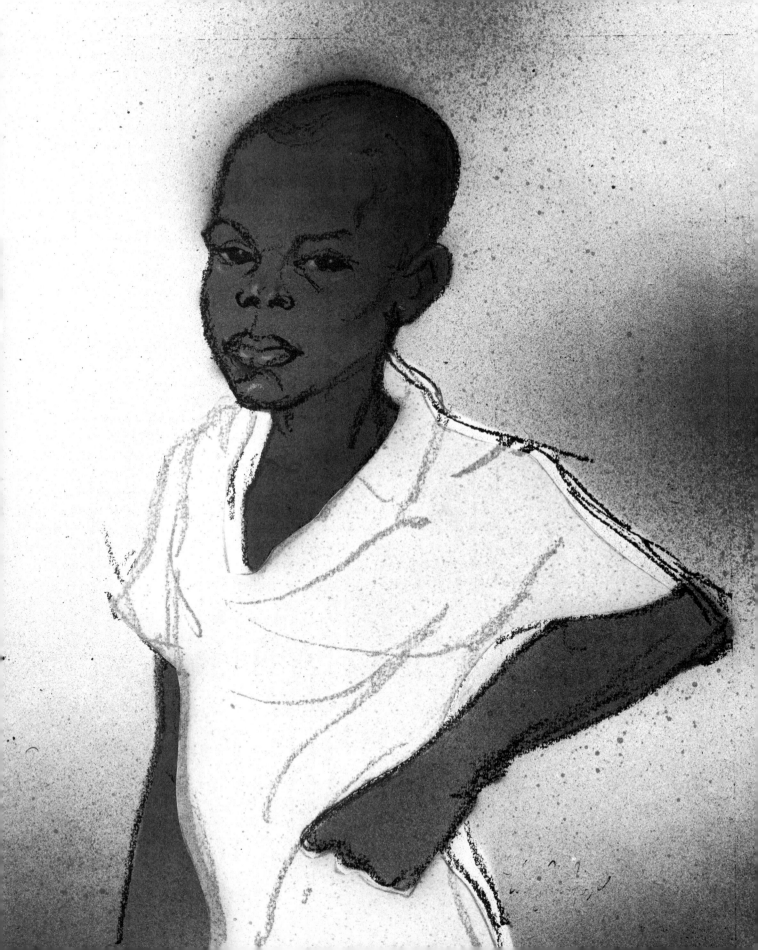

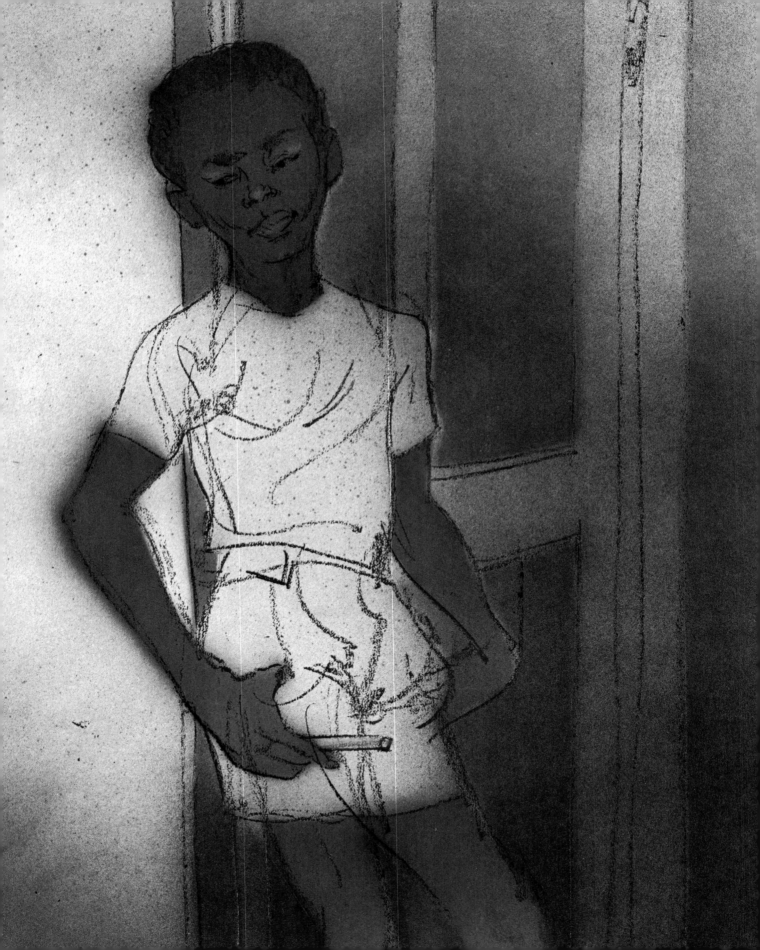

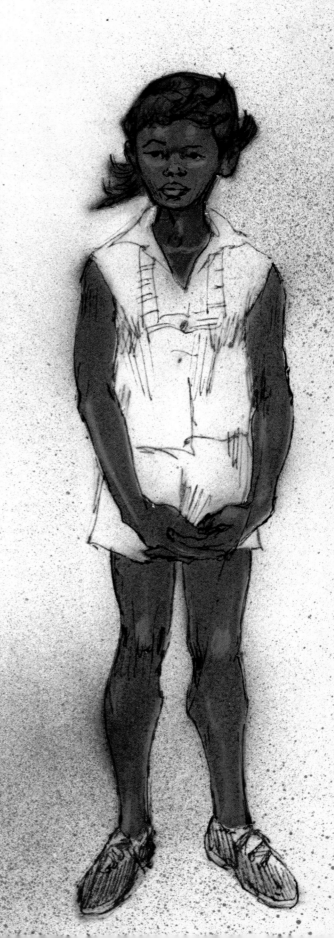

eyes turn outward,
bodies shift for action,
but for this moment they are still,

they are
the daydreamers,
letting the world dizzy itself
without them.

Scenes passing through their minds
make no sound
glide from hiding places
promenade and return
silently

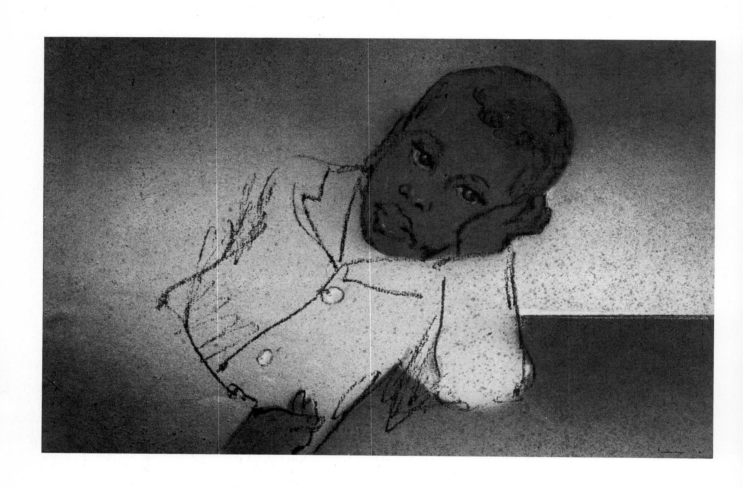

the children watch their memories
with spirit-eyes
seeing more than they saw before

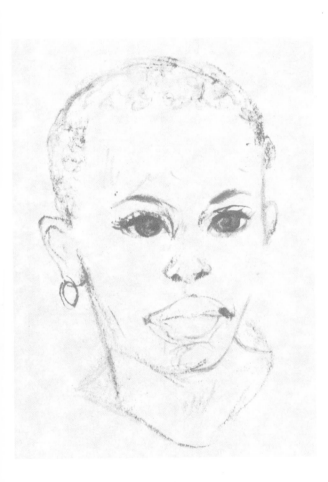

feeling more
or maybe less
than they felt the time before

reaching with spirit-hands
to touch the dreams
drawn from their yesterdays

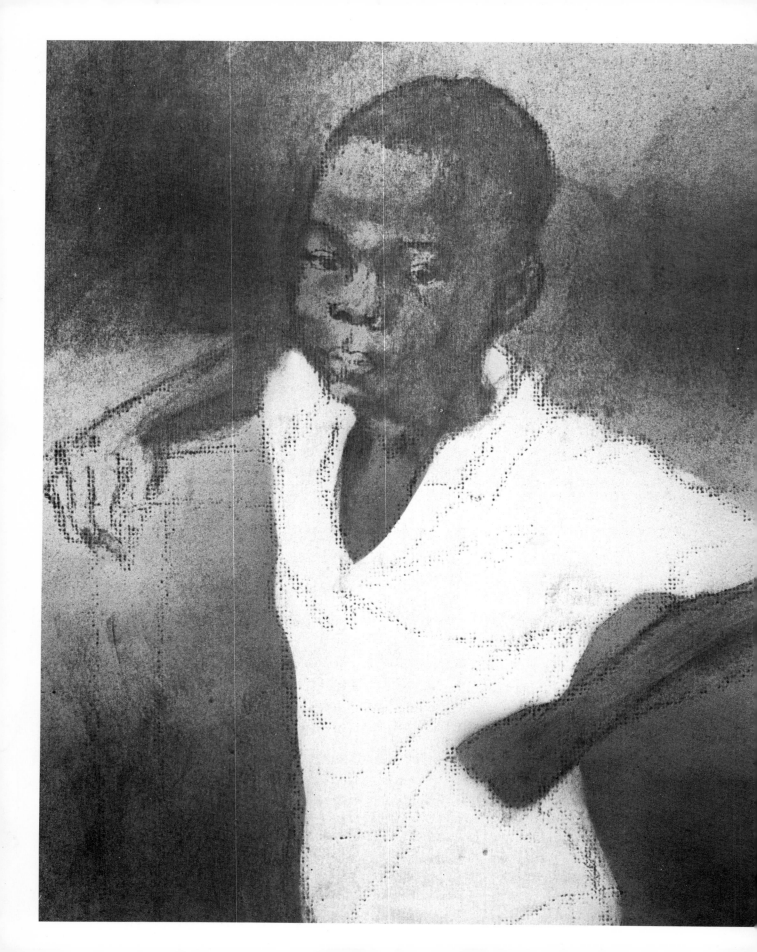

They will not be the same
after this growing time,
this dreaming.
In their stillness they have moved
forward

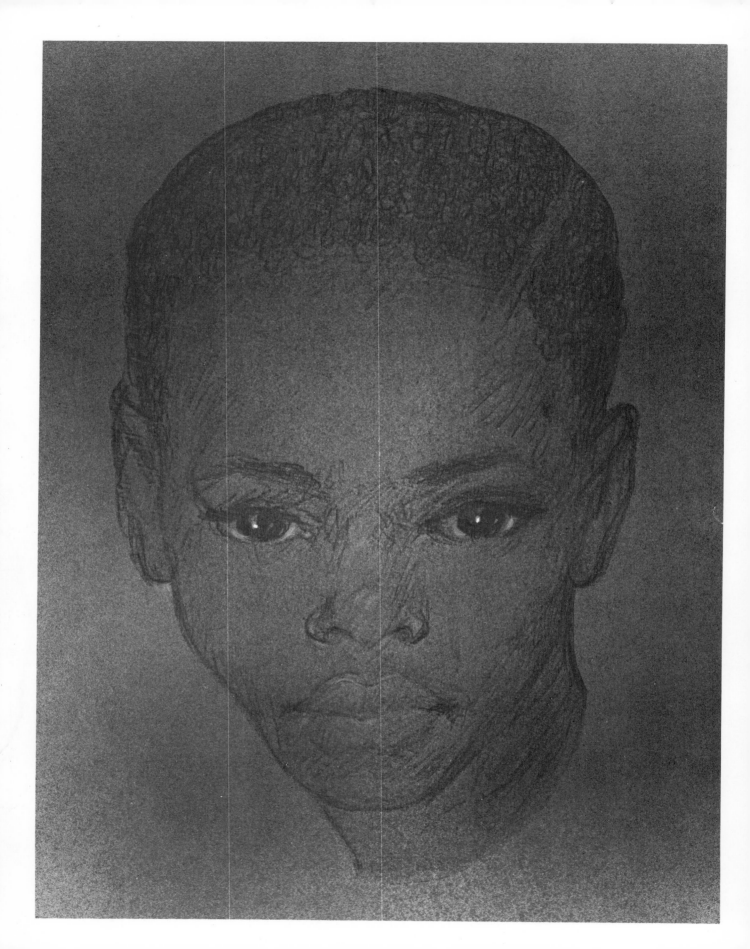

toward womanhood
toward manhood.
This dreaming has made them
new.

About the Artist

Tom Feelings is the distinguished illustrator of numerous books for young readers. He did the artwork for *To Be a Slave,* a Newbery Honor Book by Julius Lester, and has illustrated two Caldecott Honor Books, *Moja Means One: Swahili Counting Book* and *Jambo Means Hello: Swahili Alphabet Book,* both written by Muriel Feelings. His most recent book, *Something on My Mind,* with words by Nikki Grimes, received a Coretta Scott King Award for illustration and was an ALA Notable Children's Book of 1978.

Mr. Feelings was born in Brooklyn, New York, and attended the School of Visual Arts. He has lived in West Africa and Guyana, South America, where he worked in the government publishing program, training young artists in textbook illustration. He currently lives in New York City.

About the Author

Eloise Greenfield is the author of more than a dozen books for children, as well as stories and articles that have appeared in magazines such as *Ebony Jr!* and *Black World.* She was the first recipient of the Carter G. Woodson Award for her biography *Rosa Parks,* and her *Africa Dream* was the winner of the 1978 Coretta Scott King Award. Her most recent book is *Honey, I Love,* a collection of poems illustrated by Leo and Diane Dillon.

Ms. Greenfield was born in North Carolina and now lives in Washington, D.C., with her husband and family.

About the Art

The original pieces of art were prepared in pencil or pen and ink. They were then reproduced by the artist. To create greater depth and variety for the book, many of the drawings were sprayed with a transparent color dye, and others were placed against paper with a mottled design. Some of the art was printed in two colors, some in one color; all were photographed as halftone.